Lead and Let Die

Amy

Table of Contents

DEDICATION

To the dreamers and adventurers who find magic in the everyday, this book is for you. To my family and friends, whose unwavering support has been the foundation of my journey, thank you for always believing in me, even when I doubted myself. To the countless storytellers who have inspired me with their words and worlds, I am forever grateful for the stories you've shared. And to every reader who opens these pages, ready to embark on an adventure with Pencil Pete and his friends – this story exists because of you. Your passion for reading is the greatest inspiration of all.

ACKNOWLEDGMENTS

Creating Lead and Let Die has been an incredible journey, one that would not have been possible without the support and encouragement of so many wonderful people.

To my readers: Thank you from the bottom of my heart. Your enthusiasm and love for books are the true fuel behind this story. Whether you're a long-time fan or discovering my work for the first time, your willingness to step into the world of Lead and Let Die means everything to me. It's your imaginations and your willingness to believe in the unbelievable that bring this story to life. I hope that Lead and Let Die brings you as much joy and excitement as I had writing it.

To everyone who believes in the power of imagination and creativity – thank you for reminding me why we tell stories. This book is a testament to the magic that happens when we dare to dream and believe in the impossible. Here's to many more adventures together!

1 The Erasers Gambit

I knew trouble had found me again when I saw the blank space where my manuscript should have been. The emptiness mocked me, a gaping void where my words once lived. I ran my graphite-stained fingers along the smooth surface of my writing desk, searching for any trace of the pages that held my redemption.

Nothing. Not even the faintest pencil mark remained.

The tranquil life I'd carefully constructed as Graphite Gray, bestselling novelist extraordinaire, began to crumble around me. The gentle ticking of my antique clock suddenly sounded like a ticking time bomb, counting down the moments until my carefully crafted facade would explode.

I took a deep breath, trying to quell the rising panic in my chest. The peaceful existence I'd fought so hard for was slipping away faster than ink on wet paper. Images from my past life as Pencil Pete, the most feared assassin in the stationery underworld, flashed through my mind. The precise strikes, the deadly accuracy, the lives I'd ended with a single, well-placed mark.

No. I couldn't go back to that. I wouldn't.

But as I stared at the empty space where my manuscript should have been, I knew I had no choice. Someone had taken MY WORDS, MY STORY , MY TICKET to a life free from violence. And I had a sinking feeling I knew exactly who was behind it.

With a resigned sigh, I pulled open the bottom drawer of my desk. Hidden beneath a false bottom lay the tools of my former trade - sharpeners that could hone my point to a deadly edge, graphite cores that could pierce the toughest surfaces, and a collection of specialized erasers for removing all traces of evidence.

As I gathered my gear, my eyes fell on a torn scrap of paper lying on the floor near my desk. I crouched down, examining it closely. The texture was unmistakable - a unique blend of fibers used only by those operating in the shadowy corners of the stationery world. My suspicions crystalized into certainty.

Paperclip Paul. That twisted piece of bent metal was behind this.

I stood, a familiar tension coiling through my body. It had been years since I'd allowed myself to feel this way, to embrace the predatory instincts that once made me the most feared writing implement in the business. But if Paul wanted to drag me back into that world, he'd soon remember why they called me the Gray Ghost.

I slipped out of my cozy writing nook, leaving behind the facade of Graphite Gray. With each step, I felt Pencil Pete re-emerging, my senses sharpening as I prepared for the hunt ahead. The quiet streets of my neighborhood seemed alien now, potential threats lurking behind every manicured hedge and picket fence.

My first stop was clear. If anyone knew what Paul was up to, it would be Glue Gun Gary. The reformed enforcer ran a rehabilitation center for ex-cons looking to stick to the straight and narrow. Our history was complicated, to say the least, but if there was one thing I could count on, it was Gary's unbreakable bond when it came to friendship.

I found Gary's place easily enough - an old warehouse on the outskirts of town, its walls plastered with motivational posters about second chances and finding your true adhesive strength. As I approached the entrance, a gruff voice called out from the shadows.

"Well, well. Look what the eraser dragged in." Gary emerged, his nozzle gleaming in the dim light. "Didn't expect to see you darkening my doorstep again, Pete. Thought you'd gone all highbrow on us with your fancy books."

I couldn't help but smirk. "Missed you too, you old glue stick. But I'm afraid this isn't a social call."

Gary's expression hardened. "Paul?"

I nodded grimly. "He's made his move. Stole my latest manuscript."

"Damn," Gary muttered. "I'd heard whispers he was planning something big, but this... Come on inside. We've got a lot to talk about."

As we entered the warehouse, I couldn't shake the feeling that I was walking back into a world I'd tried so hard to leave behind. But with my manuscript - and my very identity - at stake, I knew there was no turning back now.

Gary led me through a maze of workstations where various writing implements and office supplies were learning new trades. A stapler was practicing yoga, stretching its metal arms in ways I didn't think possible. A stack of sticky notes was taking a meditation class, their yellow surface rippling with each deep breath.

We finally reached Gary's office, a small room cluttered with motivational knick-knacks and certificates of achievement. He gestured for me to take a seat while he paced, his nozzle twitching with agitation.

"Paul's been consolidating power," Gary explained, his voice low and gravelly. "Word on the street is he's got some grand plan to control all the documents in our world. Your manuscript must be a key piece of that puzzle."

I leaned forward, my point scraping against the worn wooden desk. "Any idea where he might be keeping it?"

Gary shook his head. "Not exactly, but I've got a lead on one of his top enforcers. Whiteout Wendy. She's been spotted hanging around an old classroom on the east side. Rumor has it there's a black-market deal going down there tonight."

I felt a familiar rush of adrenaline course through me. "Looks like we've got a date with destiny then."

Gary's eyes narrowed. "We? Who said anything about we?"

I stood, my resolve hardening. "Come on, Gary. You know you can't resist a chance to stick it to Paul. Besides, I could use someone to watch my back."

For a moment, I thought he might refuse. Then a slow grin spread across his face. "Ah, what the hell. It'll be just like old times. Let me grab my gear."

As Gary gathered his supplies, I couldn't help but feel a mix of excitement and dread. The thrill of the hunt was intoxicating, but I knew the cost all too well. Every step back into this world was a step away from the peace I'd fought so hard to achieve.

But with my manuscript - and my very identity - at stake, I had no choice. It was time for Pencil Pete to sharpen his point and show the world he still had some lead left in him.

The abandoned classroom loomed before us, a hulking shadow in the fading twilight. Gary and I crouched behind a dumpster, surveying the scene. Two burly erasers stood guard at the entrance, their rubber surfaces gleaming menacingly.

"You take left, I'll take right?" Gary whispered, his nozzle already heating up.

I nodded, feeling the familiar rush of pre-battle focus. "Just like old times."

We moved in perfect sync, years of partnership flooding back in an instant. I darted towards the left guard, my sharpened point a blur of motion. Before the eraser could even react, I'd struck three precise blows, reducing him to a pile of rubber shavings.

Gary, meanwhile, had unleashed a devastating spray of adhesive, pinning the right guard to the wall. The eraser struggled fruitlessly, his muffled curses barely audible through the layer of glue.

"Still got it, old friend," I grinned, feeling a twinge of guilt at how good it felt to be back in action.

Gary just grunted in response, but I could see the gleam of satisfaction in his eyes. We made our way into the classroom, senses on high alert.

The room was dimly lit, the faint glow of a single desk lamp casting long shadows across the dusty floor. And there, in the center of it all, stood Whiteout Wendy.

She was every bit as fearsome as I remembered - a sleek bottle of correction fluid with a nozzle that could erase a pencil mark from fifty paces. Her cold eyes narrowed as she spotted us.

"Well, well," she drawled, her voice dripping with venom. "If it isn't the prodigal pencil and his sticky sidekick. Come to crash our little party?"

I took a step forward, my point glinting in the low light. "Cut the small talk, Wendy. Where's my manuscript?"

She laughed, a harsh sound that sent shivers down my spine. "Oh, honey. You really think I'm going to just tell you? You've gone soft in your retirement."

With lightning speed, Wendy uncapped her nozzle and unleashed a blast of white fluid. I dove to the side, feeling the searing heat as it barely missed me. Where the liquid touched, it began to dissolve everything in its path.

"Gary, watch out!" I yelled, rolling to my feet.

But Gary was already in motion, firing globs of adhesive to create barriers against Wendy's corrosive attacks. The air filled with the acrid smell of chemicals as white and clear liquids collided.

I ducked behind an overturned desk, my mind racing. We needed to end this quickly before Wendy could call for backup. That's when I spotted it - a fire alarm on the far wall.

"Gary!" I shouted over the chaos. "Cover me!"

Without waiting for a response, I sprinted across the room. Wendy's white blasts peppered the ground behind me, eating away at the linoleum. I could feel the heat on my back as I ran, pushing my body to its limits.

Just as I reached the alarm, a glob of white struck my side. I cried out in pain as I felt my outer layer begin to dissolve. With the last of my strength, I pulled the fire alarm.

The sudden blare of sirens and rush of water from the sprinklers above caught Wendy off guard. Her white-out began to run, diluted by the water. Gary seized the opportunity, encasing her in a cocoon of quick-drying glue.

As the adrenaline faded, I slumped against the wall, clutching my injured side. Gary rushed over, concern etched on his face.

"You okay, Pete?" he asked, examining the damage.

I managed a weak smile. "Nothing a good sharpening won't fix. Did you find anything?"

Gary held up a crumpled piece of paper, somehow spared from the sprinklers. "Looks like part of your manuscript. And there's something else..."

As I took the paper from him, my eyes widened. There, hidden within my own words, was a message. A message that chilled me to my very core.

"Paul's not just after control," I whispered, the gravity of the situation hitting me. "He's trying to erase my entire existence."

Gary's expression hardened. "Then we've got no time to lose. We need to find the rest of that manuscript before it's too late."

As sirens wailed in the distance, we slipped out of the classroom and into the night. The game had changed, and the stakes were higher than ever. But one thing was certain - Pencil Pete was back, and I wasn't about to let anyone erase me without a fight.

2 A Sticky Situation

The safe house was a dingy motel room on the outskirts of town, the kind of place where the roaches checked in but never checked out. I sat at the rickety desk, poring over the fragment of my manuscript we'd recovered from Whiteout Wendy. The hidden message within sent chills down my graphite spine.

"Erase Pete. Erase past. Control future."

Gary paced behind me, his nozzle steaming with nervous energy. "I don't get it, Pete. Why's Paul so dead set on wiping you out? I mean, sure, you two had your differences back in the day, but this... this is something else."

I leaned back, wincing as the movement aggravated my partially dissolved side. "It's not just about me, Gary. It's about what I represent. A pencil that can change, that can create instead of destroy. Paul can't stand the idea that someone could leave that life behind."

"So he's going to what, use your own words against you?" Gary scoffed. "Seems a bit melodramatic, even for that bent piece of metal."

I shook my lead. "It's more than that. My manuscript... it's not just a story. It's a record, Gary. A record of everything I've seen, everything I've done. In the wrong hands..."

Understanding dawned in Gary's eyes. "It could bring down the whole stationery underworld."

"Exactly," I nodded grimly. "And Paul plans to use it to cement his control. He'll rewrite history, erase the parts he doesn't like - including me - and use the rest to blackmail anyone who stands in his way."

Gary whistled low. "Well, ain't that just a whole heap of trouble. So what's our next move, fearless leader?"

I stood, ignoring the protest of my battered body. "We need backup. Someone who can help us navigate Paul's web of lies and misdirection. Someone who always points in the right direction."

Gary's eyes widened. "You don't mean..."

I nodded, a slight smirk playing at the corners of my mouth. "That's right, old friend. It's time we paid a visit to Compass Carl."

We found Carl in his usual haunt, a dimly lit cartography shop filled with maps of both the real and imaginary worlds. The brass compass sat atop a stack of nautical charts, his needle spinning lazily as we approached.

"Peter, Gary," Carl's cultured voice rang out, tinged with both warmth and wariness. "It's been quite some time. I trust this isn't a social call?"

I stepped forward, my resolve strengthening. "I'm afraid not, Carl. We need your help. Paul's made his move, and he's got my manuscript. If we don't stop him-"

"The very fabric of our world could be altered," Carl finished, his needle quivering with excitement. "A quest to save not just a story, but the truth itself. How delightfully existential."

Gary rolled his eyes. "Can it with the philosophy, Carl. You in or not?"

Carl's surface seemed to gleam in the low light. "My dear Gary, how could I possibly refuse such an adventure? But first, we must properly equip ourselves for the journey ahead."

With a graceful pivot, Carl led us deeper into the shop. Dusty globes and frayed maps gave way to a hidden alcove filled with an assortment of navigational tools and weapons I'd never seen before.

"Behold," Carl announced with a flourish, "the fruits of my retirement. I may have left the life, but I never stopped preparing for the day it might call me back."

I watched in awe as Carl outfitted us with an array of specialized gear. Topographical camouflage that could blend seamlessly into any background. Cartographic grenades that could create instant mazes to confuse pursuers. And for me, a set of graphite-infused throwing stars that gleamed with deadly precision.

As we geared up, I couldn't help but feel a mix of excitement and trepidation. This was more than just a rescue mission for my manuscript. It was a chance to finally confront the shadows of my past and forge a new path forward.

"So," Gary piped up, testing the adhesive properties of his new high-pressure nozzle, "where to first, oh wise one?"

Carl's needle spun for a moment before locking into place with a decisive click. "East," he declared. "To the Archives."

I raised an eyebrow. "The Archives? But that's the most heavily guarded location in the stationery world. No one's successfully broken in there in decades."

A mischievous glint appeared in Carl's eyes. "Precisely why it's the perfect place for Paul to hide your manuscript. And precisely why we're going to be the ones to crack it wide open."

As we stepped out into the night, I felt a familiar thrill course through me. The hunt was on, and this time, the stakes couldn't be higher. With Gary's brawn,

Carl's brains, and my own rekindled skills, we just might stand a chance against Paul's grand design.

Little did I know, the true test of our abilities - and our loyalties - was yet to come.

The Archives loomed before us, a colossal fortress of filing cabinets and bookshelves that stretched as far as the eye could see. Floodlights swept across the perimeter, while squadrons of paperclip guards patrolled with military precision.

"Well," Gary muttered, "I guess a frontal assault is out of the question."

Carl's needle twitched in agreement. "Indeed. We'll need to be far more... creative in our approach."

I surveyed the scene, years of training kicking into overdrive. That's when I spotted it - a small drainage pipe near the eastern wall, just large enough for a pencil to squeeze through.

"There," I whispered, pointing it out to my companions. "Our way in.

I led the way towards the drainage pipe, my body instinctively shifting into stealth mode. Years of being the Gray Ghost came flooding back as I moved silently across the shadowed ground. Gary and Carl followed close behind, their own unique skills allowing them to match my quiet approach.

As we neared the pipe, a patrol of paperclip guards marched past. We froze, barely daring to breathe. I could feel Gary's adhesive warming up, ready to strike if we were spotted. But luck was on our side, and the guards moved on without noticing us.

"Alright," I whispered, eyeing the narrow opening. "I'll go first. Carl, you follow. Gary, you bring up the rear and make sure we're not followed."

Gary nodded grimly. "Just like old times, eh Pete? Crawling through the muck to do the dirty work."

I managed a wry smile. "Let's hope our luck holds better this time around."

With that, I squeezed into the pipe. The smell was atrocious, a mix of stale ink and moldy paper that made my lead want to curl. But I pressed on, inching forward through the darkness. Behind me, I could hear Carl's quiet muttering as he used his innate sense of direction to guide us through the twists and turns.

After what felt like hours, but was likely only minutes, I saw a faint light ahead. Approaching cautiously, I peered out into what appeared to be a vast storage room. Rows upon rows of filing cabinets stretched in every direction, each one potentially holding the key to our quest.

"We're in," I whispered back to my companions. "But finding the manuscript in this maze isn't going to be easy."

Carl squeezed up beside me, his brass surface glinting in the dim light. "Fear not, my graphite friend. My internal compass is attuned to more than just cardinal directions. I sense a concentration of malevolent intent... that way." He pointed towards a section of cabinets that looked no different from the rest.

Gary, bringing up the rear, grunted skeptically. "Malevolent intent? Sounds like a bunch of new-age nonsense to me."

"Nevertheless," I interjected, "it's the best lead we've got. Let's move."

We crept out of the pipe, staying low and using the cabinets for cover. The room was eerily quiet, broken only by the occasional distant sound of a guard's footsteps. As we neared the area Carl had indicated, I began to feel a strange tingling in my graphite core. Something was definitely off about this section.

Suddenly, a voice rang out, causing us all to freeze.

"Well, well, well. What do we have here?"

I turned slowly, my heart sinking as I recognized the smug tone. There, blocking our path, stood Tape Tom, his adhesive surface gleaming menacingly in the low light.

"If it isn't the prodigal pencil and his merry band of misfits," Tom sneered. "Did you really think it would be that easy to waltz in here and steal back your precious manuscript?"

I tensed, ready for a fight. "Tom. Still Paul's lapdog, I see. Why don't you step aside before things get messy?"

Tom's laugh was cold and cruel. "Oh Pete, you've gone soft in your retirement. Allow me to remind you what real mess looks like."

With lightning speed, Tom unleashed a barrage of adhesive strips. I dove to the side, feeling the rush of air as the tape narrowly missed me. Gary returned fire with his own adhesive, while Carl called out warnings and directions.

The battle was chaotic and fierce. Filing cabinets toppled as we ducked and weaved, documents scattering across the floor like confetti. I used my newly acquired graphite stars to slice through Tom's tape attacks, but for every strip I cut, two more seemed to take its place.

"We need to end this quick," Gary shouted, narrowly avoiding being mummified by a particularly viscous strand of tape. "Before the whole place comes down on our heads!"

He was right. The commotion was sure to attract more guards soon. I needed to think fast.

That's when I spotted it – a large industrial shredder in the corner of the room. A desperate plan formed in my mind.

"Carl!" I yelled. "Guide Gary's aim towards that shredder!"

Carl's needle spun rapidly as he assessed the situation. "Thirty degrees to your left, Gary! Maximum adhesive pressure!"

Gary didn't hesitate. He unleashed a massive glob of glue, guided by Carl's precise calculations. It struck Tom dead center, sending him sliding backwards... right into the maw of the shredder.

Tom's scream of rage was cut short as the machine roared to life. Strips of shredded tape flew everywhere, and when the noise finally died down, there was no sign of our adhesive adversary.

We stood there, panting and covered in a mixture of tape residue and paper scraps. The reality of what we'd just done began to sink in.

"Well," Gary said, breaking the tense silence. "I guess you could say Tom got himself into a sticky situation."

I couldn't help but groan at the pun, even as relief flooded through me. "Come on," I said, gesturing towards the section Carl had originally indicated. "Let's find that manuscript and get out of here before-"

My words were cut off by the sudden blare of alarms. Red lights began flashing throughout the Archives, and the distant sound of running footsteps grew louder.

"Looks like our time's up," Carl observed calmly, though his needle was spinning wildly.

I gritted my teeth, frustration warring with determination. We were so close, I could feel it. But with guards closing in from all sides, our chances of escaping with the manuscript were slim to none.

"New plan," I announced, my mind racing. "Carl, can you guide us to the nearest exit?"

The compass's needle steadied, pointing decisively. "This way. But Peter, the manuscript-"

"Will have to wait," I finished grimly. "We're no good to anyone if we're caught. We'll find another way."

As we raced through the maze of filing cabinets, alarms blaring all around us, I couldn't shake the feeling that we'd just lost a crucial battle in this war. Paul was one step ahead, and time was running out.

But as I glanced at my companions – Gary, with his unwavering loyalty, and Carl, with his guiding wisdom – I felt a spark of hope. We'd faced impossible odds before and come out on top. This time would be no different.

The Archives might have defeated us today, but Pencil Pete wasn't about to let his story end here. Not by a long shot.

3 The Price Of Redemption

15

The neon sign of "Eraser's Edge" flickered weakly in the twilight, casting an eerie glow over the dingy alleyway. I adjusted my worn fedora, trying to shake off the feeling that I was being watched. Old habits die hard, I guess.

"You sure about this, Pete?" Glue Gun Gary's gruff voice broke through my reverie. "This joint's got a reputation."

I nodded, my wooden body creaking slightly. "Paul's goons have been spotted here. We need answers, and we need 'em fast."

The ticking clock in my head wouldn't shut up. Twenty-four hours. That's all we had before Paul unleashed chaos on our world. My manuscript - my ticket to a new life - hung in the balance.

We pushed through the grimy door, the smell of cheap ink and desperation hitting us like a freight train. The bar was dimly lit, populated by the kind of stationery that usually ended up in the bottom drawer, forgotten and bitter.

A rusty paper clip behind the bar eyed us suspiciously. "We don't serve your kind here, pencil."

I leaned in, my voice low and dangerous. "I'm not here for a drink, pal. I'm looking for information."

The paper clip's eyes widened in recognition. "Wait a minute... You're him, ain't ya? Graphite Gray?"

I winced internally. So much for keeping a low profile. "That's ancient history. Now, about that information-"

A commotion from the back of the bar cut me off. Three menacing erasers, each twice my size, were making their way towards us. Their rubber bodies rippled with barely contained violence.

"Well, well," the leader sneered, his pink body covered in scars. "If it ain't the famous Pencil Pete. Heard you went soft, started scribblin' stories instead of takin' out marks."

I felt my lead grow cold. How did they know? Had Paul already started spreading the word?

Gary tensed beside me, his nozzle twitching in anticipation. "Pete, we should-"

But it was too late. The lead eraser lunged, his massive fist aimed straight for my face. I ducked, feeling the whoosh of air as it passed over my head. In one fluid motion, I spun, using my momentum to drive my sharpened tip into his midsection.

The eraser howled in pain, stumbling backward. His two buddies charged in, their rubbery arms flailing. Gary sprang into action, spraying a thick stream of adhesive at their feet. They stumbled, suddenly finding themselves stuck to the grimy floor.

I vaulted over the bar, my years of training kicking in despite my best efforts to suppress them. Grabbing a bottle of White-Out, I smashed it against the counter, creating a makeshift weapon.

"Last chance," I growled, holding the jagged bottle to the paper clip's throat. "Where's Paul hiding?"

The paper clip's eyes darted nervously. "I-I don't know nothin' about no Paul!"

A cruel laugh echoed through the bar. I turned to see a sleek fountain pen sauntering towards us, ink dripping ominously from his tip.

"Oh, Pete," he chuckled. "You always were too direct. Paul sends his regards."

Before I could react, the fountain pen flicked his wrist, sending a spray of ink directly into my eyes. I staggered back, momentarily blinded. I heard Gary shout a warning, followed by the sound of breaking glass.

Blinking furiously, I cleared my vision just in time to see Gary grappling with the fountain pen. Ink and glue flew everywhere as they traded blows. The eraser I'd stabbed earlier was back on his feet, lumbering towards me with murderous intent.

I ducked under his wild swing, using my smaller size to my advantage. Darting between his legs, I jabbed my sharpened tip into the back of his knee. He roared in pain, collapsing to the ground.

The fountain pen had Gary pinned against the wall, his inky blade pressing dangerously close to my friend's face. Without thinking, I hurled the broken White-Out bottle, watching it spin through the air before smashing into the pen's head.

He crumpled, releasing Gary. We stood there, panting, surrounded by the chaos we'd created. The bar was a mess of spilled ink, shattered glass, and groaning bodies.

"We gotta go, Pete," Gary urged, already heading for the door. "Cops'll be here any minute."

I nodded, my mind racing. We'd come for answers, but all we'd gotten was more questions. And a stark reminder of the life I'd left behind.

As we slipped out into the night, I couldn't shake the feeling that I was losing control. The carefully constructed facade of Graphite Gray was crumbling, revealing the deadly Pencil Pete underneath. And worst of all? Part of me had enjoyed it.

We made our way back to our hideout, an abandoned pencil sharpener on the outskirts of town. Compass Carl was waiting for us, his brass face creased with worry.

"What happened?" he asked, taking in our disheveled appearance.

I slumped against the wall, suddenly feeling every year of my existence. "It was a trap, Carl. They knew we were coming."

Gary nodded grimly. "Paul's got eyes everywhere. We're running out of time and options."

Carl's needle spun wildly for a moment before settling. "Perhaps... perhaps we need to consider the possibility that we've been compromised."

The words hung heavy in the air. A traitor among us? The thought made my lead run cold.

I stood up, pacing the small space. "No. I trust you both with my life. We can't start doubting each other now."

But even as I said the words, I felt the first seeds of suspicion taking root. Gary's violent past, Carl's mysterious origins... How well did I really know my allies?

The ticking clock in my head grew louder. Twenty hours left. Paul's plan was in motion, and we were no closer to stopping him. My manuscript - my chance at redemption - was slipping away.

I clenched my fists, feeling the familiar pull of my old life. The clarity that came with violence, the simplicity of a world divided into targets and obstacles. It would be so easy to slip back into that mindset, to become the weapon I was designed to be.

But that path led only to more pain, more destruction. I'd walked away from that life for a reason. I had to find another way.

"Alright," I said, forcing determination into my voice. "We need a new plan. Carl, can you use your skills to map out potential hideouts for Paul? Gary, reach out to your old contacts. Someone must know something."

They nodded, but I could see the doubt in their eyes. They were counting on me to lead them through this, and I was floundering.

As they set to work, I retreated to a corner, pulling out a crumpled sheet of paper. My hands shook slightly as I began to write, pouring my fears and doubts onto the page. It was a poor substitute for my manuscript, but it was all I had.

The words flowed, a mixture of noir-tinged observations and raw emotion. I wrote about the weight of the past, the fragility of redemption, and the fear of losing oneself. In those moments, I wasn't Pencil Pete the ex-assassin or Graphite Gray the novelist. I was just a pencil, trying to make sense of a world that seemed determined to erase me.

Hours passed, the tension in our hideout growing with each tick of the clock. We were running out of time, and I was running out of ideas. The pressure was building, threatening to snap me in two.

Little did I know, the true test was yet to come. As the first light of dawn crept through the cracks in our hideout, we received news that would change everything. Paul had made his move, and the clock wasn't just ticking anymore - it was about to explode.

4 Secrets in the artroom

The crack of dawn painted the sky in hues of orange and pink, but I couldn't appreciate the view. My wooden body ached from the previous night's brawl, and my mind raced with the possibilities of Paul's next move.

"Pete, you gotta see this," Gary's gruff voice cut through my brooding.

I made my way to the makeshift war room we'd set up in our pencil sharpener hideout. Carl was there too, his brass face reflecting the dim light of our single bulb.

"What've we got?" I asked, trying to keep the exhaustion out of my voice.

Carl's needle spun wildly before settling on a crudely drawn map. "We've triangulated Paul's possible locations based on recent criminal activity and—"

A sudden gust of wind tore through our hideout, scattering our carefully arranged notes and clues. Papers whirled around us in a frenzied dance, obscuring our vision.

"What the hell?" Gary shouted, trying to grab at the flying documents.

I lunged for a crucial piece of evidence—a receipt from Sticky's Diner with a scribbled message on the back. My fingers brushed against it, but another gust snatched it away, sucking it out through a crack in the wall.

As quickly as it started, the wind died down, leaving us in a mess of scattered papers and confusion.

"That... that wasn't natural," Carl muttered, his usual calm demeanor shaken.

I nodded grimly. "Paul's got some new tricks up his sleeve. We need to be more careful."

We spent the next hour reorganizing our intel, but the damage was done. Key pieces were missing, and our carefully constructed timeline was in shambles.

"We need more information," I declared, adjusting my fedora. "Let's hit the streets. Someone must've seen something."

We split up, each taking a different part of town. I found myself in the school district, the quiet halls a stark contrast to the chaos in my mind.

As I turned a corner, a classroom door caught my eye. It was slightly ajar, a faint light spilling out. My instincts screamed trap, but we were out of options.

I pushed the door open, my body tense and ready for action. The classroom seemed empty, rows of desks bathed in the soft glow of a forgotten desk lamp.

"Hello?" I called out, feeling foolish even as I did so.

Silence answered me. I took a step forward, my wooden body creaking slightly.

Suddenly, the room erupted into chaos. Alarms blared, lights flashed, and what I thought were ordinary desks sprang to life, revealing hidden compartments bristling with office supply weaponry.

"Damn it!" I cursed, diving behind a teacher's desk as a barrage of staples embedded themselves in the wall where I'd been standing.

The room was a death trap, and I was smack in the middle of it. Rubber bands whizzed past my head, scissors snapped menacingly in the air, and I could hear the ominous whirr of a pencil sharpener warming up.

I needed an escape plan, and fast. My eyes darted around the room, looking for anything I could use. There—a fire extinguisher tucked away in the corner.

Taking a deep breath, I made a mad dash across the room. Staples and rubber bands assaulted me from all sides. One rubber band caught me across the face, leaving a stinging welt, but I pushed through the pain.

Grabbing the extinguisher, I turned and unleashed a cloud of white foam across the room. The automated defenses sputtered and choked, giving me the opening I needed.

I sprinted for the door, my heart pounding in my wooden chest. Just as I reached the threshold, I felt something wrap around my ankle. Looking down, I saw a length of measuring tape, pulling me back into the chaos.

With a grunt of effort, I drove my sharpened tip into the tape, severing it. Freedom was just steps away.

I burst out of the classroom, slamming the door behind me. The alarms continued to blare, but they sounded muffled now, like a distant nightmare.

Leaning against the wall, I tried to catch my breath. What the hell was that? How did Paul know I'd be here?

The sound of approaching footsteps snapped me back to reality. I couldn't stick around to find out if they were friend or foe.

I made my way out of the school, my mind reeling from the close call. This was more than just Paul flexing his power. This was calculated, precise. He was always one step ahead of us.

As I rendezvoused with Gary and Carl at our predetermined meeting spot, I could see similar expressions of frustration and fear on their faces.

"You too, huh?" Gary grunted, nursing a nasty paper cut on his nozzle.

Carl's usually stoic face was creased with worry. "These... occurrences. They're not random. Someone's feeding Paul information about our movements."

The word hung unspoken between us. Traitor.

I shook my head, trying to dispel the growing paranoia. "Let's focus on what we know. Paul's getting bolder, which means he's close to making his big move. We need to strike first."

Gary cracked his knuckles, a dangerous glint in his eye. "I might know a guy who can help. Goes by the name Tape Tom. He's one of Paul's enforcers, but he's got a weakness for shiny things. If we can get him alone..."

I nodded, a plan already forming in my mind. "The school's art room. Lots of glittery projects, easy to get lost in. It's perfect."

As we hashed out the details of our plan, I couldn't shake the feeling that we were walking into another trap. But what choice did we have? The clock was ticking, and Paul's endgame was approaching fast.

Little did I know, our confrontation with Tape Tom would change everything. The art room would become a battlefield, and the revelations that followed would shake us to our very core.

But that's a tale for another time. Right now, we had a date with danger, and I intended to look my best. I straightened my fedora, checked my lead, and steeled myself for what was to come.

"Let's go catch ourselves a rat," I growled, leading our little band of misfits into the unknown.

The sun was setting as we made our way to the school, casting long shadows that seemed to reach for us with grasping fingers. The art room waited, a crucible where loyalties would be tested and truths revealed.

One way or another, this night would end with answers. Whether we'd like what we found... well, that was another matter entirely.

5 The ticking clock

I never thought I'd miss the simplicity of my old life as an assassin. Back then, it was just me, my target, and the satisfying scratch of graphite on paper as I crossed another name off my list. Now? Now I'm stuck in a pressure cooker, and the heat's cranking up by the second.

The clock on my desk ticks away, each movement of its hands like a hammer blow to my already frayed nerves. Tick. Tock. Tick. Tock. The sound mingles with the furious tapping of my eraser on the wooden surface. I've been staring at the same blank page for hours, willing the words to come, but my mind's a jumble of worst-case scenarios and half-baked plans.

"Get it together, Pete," I mutter, running a hand over my worn-down tip. "You've faced worse than this."

But have I? The stakes have never been higher. It's not just my life on the line anymore. It's Gary's. Carl's. Hell, the entire stationery world could come crashing down if I don't figure out how to stop Paul.

A knock at the door jolts me from my spiral. I'm on my feet in an instant, years of training kicking in as I slide silently across the room. My grip tightens on a nearby letter opener – not my weapon of choice, but it'll do in a pinch.

"Pete? It's me, open up!"

Gary's gruff voice filters through the wood, and I let out a breath I didn't realize I was holding. I unlock the door, ushering him inside quickly before scanning the hallway. All clear. For now.

"You look like hell, pal," Gary says, his nozzle creasing with concern. "When's the last time you got some shut-eye?"

I wave off his worry, collapsing back into my chair. "Sleep's a luxury we can't afford right now. What's the word on the street?"

Gary's expression darkens, and I feel my gut clench. Bad news incoming.

"It's not good, Pete. Paul's men are everywhere. They hit my rehab center last night."

"Damn it!" I slam my fist on the desk, sending papers flying. "Anyone hurt?"

Gary shakes his head. "Nah, we got lucky. Managed to evacuate everyone before they torched the place. But it's a message, loud and clear. Paul's not playing around anymore."

I nod, my mind racing. "And Carl? Have you heard from him?"

The silence that follows is deafening. Gary won't meet my eyes, and I feel a cold dread seeping into my core.

"Gary. What happened to Carl?"

He sighs, his shoulders sagging. "He was on his way to meet you yesterday. Never showed up. I've got my contacts out looking, but..."

The rest goes unsaid. We both know what it means when someone disappears in our world. I close my eyes, fighting back the wave of guilt threatening to drown me. Carl, with his infinite wisdom and unwavering moral compass. He didn't deserve to be caught up in this mess.

"We'll find him," I say, more to convince myself than Gary. "Paul wouldn't... he needs information. Carl's alive."

Gary nods, but the doubt in his eyes mirrors my own. We stand in silence for a moment, the weight of the situation pressing down on us like a ton of bricks.

"So, what's the plan, boss?" Gary asks, breaking the tension. "We can't just sit around waiting for Paul's next move."

He's right, of course. But the truth is, I'm running out of ideas. Every lead we've followed has turned into a dead end. Every step forward has been met with two steps back. For the first time in my life, I'm starting to wonder if I'm outmatched.

"I need to finish the manuscript," I say finally, gesturing to the blank page mocking me from the desk. "It's the only leverage we have left. If I can just..."

My words trail off as I notice Gary's expression. He's not looking at me anymore, his gaze fixed on something behind me. I spin around, following his line of sight to the recovered manuscript piece pinned to my corkboard.

"Pete," Gary says slowly, "has that always been there?"

I frown, stepping closer to examine the paper. "What are you talking about? It's just the piece we..."

And then I see it. Faint lines, almost invisible to the naked eye, crisscrossing the text. My heart starts racing as I trace the pattern with my finger.

"It's a map," I breathe, hardly daring to believe it. "Gary, it's a goddamn map!"

The next few hours are a blur of activity. We pore over the manuscript, decoding the hidden message within its pages. It's intricate work, requiring every ounce of concentration I can muster. But with each line we decipher, a picture begins to emerge.

"This is it," I say, my voice hoarse from hours of discussion. "This has to be Paul's hideout."

Gary leans in, studying the crude map we've managed to piece together. "Are you sure? It could be another trap."

I shake my head, a fire igniting in my core. "No, this feels right. Paul's ego wouldn't let him resist leaving a breadcrumb trail. He wants us to find him, to walk right into his clutches."

"So, we're just gonna give him what he wants?" Gary asks, skepticism clear in his tone.

A grim smile spreads across my face. "Oh, we're going to give him exactly what he wants. And then some."

We spend the next few hours planning, strategizing every possible angle. Gary reaches out to his contacts, gathering intel on the warehouse district where Paul's lair is supposedly hidden. I dust off my old gear, the familiar weight of my tactical belt a comfort I didn't realize I'd missed.

As the sun begins to set, casting long shadows across my apartment, we make our final preparations. Gary's nozzle is primed and ready, extra glue sticks tucked into every available pocket. I run my finger along my sharpened tip, relishing the lethal point I've honed to perfection.

"One thing I don't get," Gary says as we gear up. "Where's Carl in all this? If Paul has him, why isn't he mentioned in the map?"

It's a question that's been nagging at me too, but I push it aside. "We'll find out soon enough. For now, we focus on the mission. You ready?"

Gary nods, a steely determination in his eyes. "Born ready, partner."

We slip out of the apartment under the cover of darkness, two shadows moving silently through the city streets. The warehouse district looms ahead, a maze of abandoned buildings and rusted metal. The perfect place for a criminal mastermind to set up shop.

As we approach our target, I can't shake the feeling that we're walking into something bigger than we realize. But there's no turning back now. Paul has pushed us to the brink, threatened everything and everyone I care about. It's time to end this, one way or another.

"Remember the plan," I whisper to Gary as we take up positions outside the warehouse. "We go in hard and fast. Neutralize any threats, but Paul is mine."

Gary gives me a curt nod, his grip tightening on his nozzle. "Just like old times, eh?"

I allow myself a small smile. "Let's hope not. I like to think we've learned a thing or two since then."

With a deep breath, I signal the go-ahead. Gary moves first, spraying a glob of adhesive at the lock. It sizzles and melts, the door swinging open with an ominous creak. We're in.

The warehouse is a labyrinth of shipping containers and scaffolding, creating a multi-level playground for Paul's minions. And they're everywhere. Paperclips of all sizes, their pointed ends gleaming in the dim light. They move with military precision, clearly well-trained and ready for a fight.

We don't give them a chance to raise the alarm. I dart forward, my sharpened tip finding vulnerable spots with deadly accuracy. One, two, three paperclips fall before they even realize what's happening. Gary's right behind me, his adhesive spray creating chaos in the ranks.

But Paul's forces are numerous, and soon the element of surprise is gone. The warehouse erupts into a cacophony of clanging metal and shouted orders. We're outnumbered, outgunned, and fighting on unfamiliar terrain.

In other words, it's a typical Tuesday for Pencil Pete.

I duck behind a stack of crates as a barrage of staples whizzes past my head. "Gary! We need to thin them out!"

He grunts in acknowledgment, popping up from his cover to lay down a wide spray of glue. It catches several paperclips mid-leap, leaving them struggling uselessly against the sticky restraints.

I take advantage of the opening, vaulting over my hiding spot and into the fray. My world narrows to a series of lightning-fast exchanges – dodge, parry, strike. My tip finds its mark again and again, leaving a trail of incapacitated foes in my wake.

But for every paperclip we take down, two more seem to appear. They're herding us, I realize with growing dread. Pushing us deeper into the warehouse, away from any hope of escape.

"Pete! On your six!"

Gary's warning comes just in time. I spin, narrowly avoiding the business end of a particularly nasty-looking paperclip. He's bigger than the others, probably one of Paul's lieutenants. His pointed end gleams with a wicked sharpness that would put most pencils to shame.

"Well, well," he sneers, circling me slowly. "The famous Pencil Pete. Not so tough without your fancy words to hide behind, are you?"

I match his movements, keeping my guard up. "Why don't you come a little closer and find out?"

He lunges, surprisingly fast for his size. But I'm faster. I sidestep his attack, using his momentum against him to send him crashing into a nearby container. He recovers quickly, though, and we're soon locked in a deadly dance.

Block, counter, dodge. The clash of metal on graphite echoes through the warehouse. He's good, I'll give him that. But I've got years of experience and the desperation of a cornered animal on my side.

Finally, I see my opening. As he overextends on a particularly vicious swipe, I drop low and drive my point up and under his guard. There's a moment of resistance, and then... release. The paperclip's eyes go wide with shock, his form already beginning to uncurl.

"That's the thing about us pencils," I pant, watching him collapse. "We might make mistakes, but we always leave our mark."

There's no time to savor the victory. Gary's shout draws my attention to the upper levels, where a fresh wave of attackers is pouring in. We're running out of time and options.

"Pete! This way!"

I follow Gary's voice, weaving through the chaos toward a small side door. It's our best shot at regrouping, maybe finding a way to turn the tables. But as we burst through into a dimly lit corridor, I can't shake the feeling that we're playing right into Paul's hands.

The hallway stretches out before us, a straight shot to what can only be the heart of Paul's operation. It's too easy, too convenient. Every instinct screams that it's a trap.

But what choice do we have?

"You thinking what I'm thinking?" Gary asks, his nozzle aimed at the door behind us.

I nod grimly. "Spring the trap."

With a determined set to his shoulders, Gary seals the door shut with a thick layer of adhesive. It won't hold them forever, but it'll buy us some time. We turn as one, facing the long corridor and whatever lies at its end.

"Ready to end this?" I ask, allowing myself a small smirk.

Gary matches my expression, his grip tightening on his weapon. "Born ready, partner."

We move forward, every sense on high alert. The sound of pursuit fades behind us, replaced by an eerie silence. Our footsteps echo off the metal walls, each one bringing us closer to our final confrontation with Paperclip Paul.

As we reach the end of the hallway, a massive set of double doors looms before us. This is it. The point of no return. I share a quick glance with Gary, seeing my own determination reflected in his eyes.

With a deep breath, I reach out and push the doors open.

The room beyond is bathed in shadows, lit only by the eerie glow of computer screens. And there, silhouetted against the largest monitor, stands the unmistakable form of Paperclip Paul.

"Ah, Pencil Pete," his voice drips with false warmth. "So good of you to join us. I've been expecting you."

As my eyes adjust to the dim light, I feel my blood run cold. Because Paul isn't alone. Tied to a chair in the center of the room, looking worse for wear but mercifully alive, is Compass Carl.

"Let him go, Paul," I growl, my tip itching for a fight. "This is between you and me."

Paul's laughter echoes off the walls, setting my teeth on edge. "Oh, Pete. You still don't get it, do you? This was never just about you."

With a theatrical flourish, he gestures to the bank of computers behind him. Images flash across the screens – schematics, blueprints, lists of names. My eyes widen as I begin to understand the scope of what I'm seeing.

"You see," Paul continues, practically preening, "while you've been running around playing hero, I've been busy. This little hideout? It's just the tip of the iceberg."

The truth hits me like a punch to the gut. We've been played. All of it – the manuscript, the map, this entire confrontation – it's all been a distraction.

"What have you done, Paul?" I ask, dreading the answer.

His grin widens, a predatory gleam in his eye. "I've done what you never had the vision to accomplish, Pete. I've reshaped the world. And now, thanks to you, I have everything I need to finish the job."

As the weight of his words sinks in, I realize with growing horror that we've walked right into Paul's endgame. And the real battle? It's only just beginning.

6 Final Gambit

31

The room feels like it's closing in on me, the weight of Paul's revelation pressing down on my shoulders. I've been played like a cheap fiddle, and the consequences are unfolding before my eyes.

"You're bluffing," I say, but the tremor in my voice betrays my uncertainty.

Paul's smile widens, his metallic form gleaming in the low light. "Am I, Pete? Take a closer look."

He gestures to the screens behind him, and I force myself to focus. The schematics, the blueprints – they're not just random plans. They're a roadmap to dismantling everything we've built in the stationery world. Supply chains, distribution networks, even the delicate balance of power between different factions. Paul hasn't just been planning a takeover; he's orchestrating a complete revolution.

"You see," Paul continues, practically giddy with self-satisfaction, "while you've been chasing your tail, I've been laying the groundwork for a new world order. One where information is power, and I control it all."

Gary shifts beside me, his nozzle trained on Paul. "So what's stopping us from ending this right now, huh? We've got you outnumbered."

Paul's laughter sends a chill down my spine. "Outnumbered? Oh, my dear glue gun, you have no idea."

With a snap of his metallic body, the shadows around us come to life. Paperclips of all sizes emerge from hidden corners, their pointed ends glinting menacingly. We're surrounded, outgunned, and completely at Paul's mercy.

"Now then," Paul says, his tone suddenly businesslike, "let's discuss terms, shall we?"

I glance at Carl, still bound and gagged in the center of the room. His eyes meet mine, and I can see a mixture of fear and determination in them. Whatever happens, I can't let Paul win.

"What do you want, Paul?" I ask, buying time as I frantically try to come up with a plan.

He begins to pace, his movements deliberately slow and measured. "It's quite simple, really. I want your manuscript, Pete. The full, unaltered version. With it, I can complete my collection of sensitive information and truly consolidate my power."

I scoff, trying to mask my growing dread. "And why would I give that to you?"

Paul's smile turns predatory. "Because if you don't, I'll start by erasing your friend Carl here. Then I'll move on to Gary, and then every other piece of stationery that's ever meant anything to you. I'll wipe out your entire world, Pete, and make you watch as I do it."

The threat hangs in the air, heavy and suffocating. I can feel Gary tensing beside me, ready for action. But any move we make could spell disaster for Carl.

"You're insane," I spit out, buying more time. "Even if I gave you the manuscript, you'd never get away with this. The other factions won't stand for it."

Paul's laugh is cold and mirthless. "Oh, Pete. Always thinking so small. Why do you think I let you find this place? Why do you think I laid out such an obvious trail?"

The realization hits me like a ton of bricks. "This isn't your real hideout."

"Give the pencil a prize!" Paul crows. "This? This is just a decoy. A carefully constructed stage for our little drama. My real operation? It's somewhere you'd never think to look."

My mind races, trying to piece together the puzzle. Where would Paul hide something so massive that even I couldn't find it? And then it hits me, a cold dread settling in my gut.

"My old hideout," I whisper, the words barely audible.

Paul's eyes gleam with triumph. "Bingo! The last place anyone would think to look for me is right under your nose. Poetic, isn't it?"

I feel like I've been sucker-punched. My old hideout, the place where I stored all my deepest secrets, the last remnants of my life as an assassin. Paul's been operating right under my nose this whole time.

"Why are you telling us this?" Gary growls, his adhesive nozzle trembling with barely contained rage.

Paul shrugs, the gesture almost casual. "Because in about five minutes, it won't matter. My plan is already in motion. This little confrontation? It's just the cherry on top."

I lock eyes with Gary, a silent understanding passing between us. We're out of options. It's time for something drastic.

"Well then," I say, straightening to my full height, "I guess there's only one thing left to do."

In one fluid motion, I launch myself at Paul. The room erupts into chaos. Gary lets loose with a barrage of adhesive, catching several paperclips in the sticky spray. I dodge and weave through the melee, my sharpened tip seeking its target.

Paul's faster than I expected, his metallic form bending and twisting to avoid my strikes. We dance a deadly waltz around the room, trading blows and near-misses.

"You're slipping, Pete!" Paul taunts as he narrowly avoids another of my attacks. "All those years of soft living have made you weak!"

I grit my teeth, pushing myself harder. He's right, in a way. I'm not the cold-blooded killer I once was. But that's not weakness – it's growth.

"You're wrong, Paul," I pant, parrying one of his jabs. "I'm stronger than I've ever been. Because now? I have something worth fighting for."

Our battle takes us across the room, smashing into computer banks and scattering paperclips in our wake. From the corner of my eye, I can see Gary holding his own against a swarm of attackers, his adhesive creating a defensive perimeter around Carl.

But we're outnumbered and outgunned. For every paperclip we take down, two more seem to appear. Time is running out.

In a desperate move, I feint left and then drive forward with all my might. My tip finds its mark, scoring a deep gash along Paul's side. He howls in pain and rage, his form bending at an unnatural angle.

"You'll pay for that, you graphite goon!" he snarls, his eyes blazing with hatred.

Before I can press my advantage, a sharp pain explodes in my side. One of Paul's minions has flanked me, its pointed end buried deep in my wooden body. I stagger, momentarily stunned by the agony.

Paul seizes the opportunity, launching himself at me with renewed fury. We crash to the ground in a tangle of limbs and sharp edges. I can feel my strength ebbing, the wound in my side sapping my energy.

"It's over, Pete," Paul hisses, his face inches from mine. "You've lost. Everything you've built, everything you care about – it's all going to crumble. And you'll live just long enough to see it happen."

As darkness starts to creep in at the edges of my vision, I hear Gary's desperate shout. "Pete! Hang on, buddy!"

But Paul's minions have him pinned down, unable to reach me. This is it, I realize with a sinking feeling. This is how Pencil Pete meets his end.

And then, just as I'm about to give in to the encroaching darkness, a familiar voice cuts through the chaos.

"Not today, you twisted paper pusher!"

There's a blinding flash of light, and suddenly Paul is wrenched away from me. I blink, trying to clear my vision, and what I see makes my heart soar.

Compass Carl stands tall, his bindings shredded at his feet. His needle glows with an otherworldly light, pointing directly at Paul.

"How..." Paul sputters, his cool demeanor finally cracking. "You were tied up! Helpless!"

Carl's laugh is warm and rich, a stark contrast to the cold chaos around us. "Oh, Paul. You of all people should know – a good compass always finds its way."

With a flick of his wrist, Carl sends a burst of energy pulsing through the room. Paul's minions scatter, their formation broken. Gary seizes the opportunity, laying down cover fire with his adhesive spray.

I struggle to my feet, ignoring the burning pain in my side. This is our chance, maybe our only one.

"Carl," I gasp, "the computers. We need to..."

He nods, understanding immediately. While Gary and I hold off the remaining paperclips, Carl makes his way to the bank of screens. His needle glows brighter as he touches each monitor, corrupting the data with bursts of magnetic energy.

Paul's anguished cry echoes through the room as his carefully laid plans literally go up in smoke. "No! Do you have any idea what you've done?!"

I allow myself a grim smile. "Saved the world, I'd say. Or at least bought it some time."

With a roar of pure rage, Paul launches himself at Carl. But he's not thinking clearly anymore, his moves sloppy and predictable. I intercept him mid-air, driving my sharpened tip deep into his metallic body.

For a moment, time seems to stand still. Paul's eyes widen in shock and disbelief. Then, with a final, rattling gasp, he goes limp.

The remaining paperclips, seeing their leader fall, quickly surrender. Gary makes short work of restraining them with his adhesive.

As the adrenaline fades, the full weight of what we've accomplished starts to sink in. We've stopped Paul's immediate plan, but the threat is far from over.

"We need to move," I say, wincing as I probe the wound in my side. "Paul's real hideout is still out there, and who knows what failsafes he has in place."

Carl nods, his glow dimming as he powers down. "I managed to extract some information from the computers before I fried them. It's not much, but it should give us a starting point."

Gary finishes securing the last of the paperclips and joins us. "So, we're heading to your old digs, Pete? Gotta say, I'm curious to see where the legendary Pencil Pete got his start."

I can't help but chuckle, despite the gravity of the situation. "Trust me, it's not as glamorous as you're imagining. But yeah, that's our next stop. We need to end this once and for all."

As we make our way out of the decoy hideout, I can't shake the feeling that we're walking into something even bigger than we realize. My old hideout holds more than just memories – it holds secrets that I've spent years trying to forget.

But there's no turning back now. Paul might be down, but his plan is still in motion. And the only way to stop it is to confront my past head-on.

The streets are eerily quiet as we make our way across town. It's as if the entire stationery world is holding its breath, waiting to see how this will all play out.

"So, what exactly are we walking into here, Pete?" Gary asks as we near our destination. "I mean, I know you were a big shot back in the day, but..."

I sigh, the weight of my past pressing down on me. "It's... complicated. My old hideout wasn't just a base of operations. It was a vault of sorts. Every piece of sensitive information I gathered during my assassin days, every secret that could topple governments or rewrite history – it's all there."

Carl's needle twitches, picking up on the tension in my voice. "And you think Paul's found a way to access it all?"

I nod grimly. "If he's been operating out of there, he's had plenty of time to crack my security measures. We have to assume he has full access to everything."

The implications hang heavy in the air. With that kind of information at his disposal, Paul could reshape the entire world, not just the stationery community.

As we round the final corner, I feel my heart skip a beat. The old warehouse that houses my former hideout looks exactly as I left it years ago – a nondescript building that no one would look at twice. But now, knowing what lurks inside, it feels like a powder keg ready to explode.

"Alright," I say, steeling myself for what's to come. "We go in quiet. No telling what kind of security Paul's set up. Gary, you take point. Carl, watch our six. I'll guide us through the layout."

They nod, falling into formation with practiced ease. As we approach the entrance, I can't help but feel a sense of déjà vu. How many times had I slipped in and out of this place, my hands stained with the metaphorical blood of my targets?

The door opens with a soft click – my old access code still works. We slip inside, every sense on high alert. The main floor is dark and seemingly deserted, but I know better than to trust appearances.

"This way," I whisper, leading them towards a hidden panel in the far wall. "The real hideout is underground."

As we descend the secret staircase, the air grows thick with tension. Each step brings us closer to a confrontation that could change everything.

The basement level is a stark contrast to the abandoned warehouse above. Banks of computers line the walls, their screens casting an eerie blue glow over the room. In the center, a massive holographic display flickers to life as we enter.

"Welcome home, Pencil Pete," a familiar voice echoes through the space. "I've been expecting you."

My blood runs cold as the hologram takes shape. It's Paul – or rather, a digital version of him. His smug grin is even more infuriating in larger-than-life form.

"You're too late, you know," Holo-Paul continues. "Even as we speak, my plan is unfolding across the globe. Every piece of information in your precious vault is being weaponized, reshaping the world as we know it."

I grit my teeth, fighting back the wave of guilt and anger threatening to overwhelm me. "It's not too late, Paul. We'll find a way to stop this."

His laughter fills the room, cold and mirthless. "Oh, Pete. Always the optimist. But I'm afraid you're out of options this time. In fact, you've played right into my final trap."

Before we can react, steel shutters slam down over the exits. Alarms blare as a countdown appears on every screen.

"You have five minutes before this entire facility self-destructs," Holo-Paul announces with sadistic glee. "Taking with it the last hope of stopping my plan. Goodbye, Pencil Pete. It's been fun."

As the hologram fades away, we're left staring at each other in stunned silence. Five minutes to save the world. No pressure, right?

"Ideas?" Gary asks, his voice tight with tension. "Because I gotta tell you, I'm coming up empty here."

I force myself to focus, pushing aside the panic clawing at my insides. This is my turf, my old stomping grounds. There has to be a way out.

"Carl," I say, an idea starting to form. "Can you interface with the computer system? Maybe find a way to abort the self-destruct sequence?"

He nods, already moving towards the nearest terminal. "I'll do my best, but no guarantees. Paul's had a lot of time to modify your old security protocols."

As Carl works his magic, Gary and I scour the room for anything that might help. But every cabinet, every drawer is empty. Paul's been thorough in his preparations.

"Three minutes," the computerized voice announces, sending a fresh wave of urgency through us.

"Pete!" Carl calls out, his voice strained. "I've managed to access some of the system, but I can't stop the countdown. There's some kind of physical failsafe."

My mind races, trying to remember every detail of this place. And then it hits me.

"The vault," I breathe. "There's a manual override in the main vault. It's where I kept my most sensitive information."

Gary's eyes widen. "Well, what are we waiting for? Let's go!"

We race through the facility, the countdown echoing in our ears. Two minutes left. The vault door looms before us, a massive steel barrier designed to withstand anything short of a nuclear blast.

"The code," I mutter, my hands shaking as I input the sequence. "Come on, come on..."

With a hiss of hydraulics, the door swings open. We rush inside, and I head straight for the hidden panel in the back wall.

"One minute remaining," the computer helpfully informs us.

I yank open the panel, revealing a complex array of switches and buttons. This is it – our last hope.

"Pete," Gary says, his voice uncharacteristically gentle. "Whatever happens... it's been an honor, partner."

I nod, not trusting myself to speak. With a deep breath, I start the override sequence. Lights flash, alarms blare, and for a heart-stopping moment, I think we've failed.

And then... silence.

The countdown freezes with just seconds to spare. We stand there, hardly daring to breathe, waiting for the other shoe to drop.

"Self-destruct sequence aborted," the computer announces, and I feel my knees go weak with relief.

We did it. We actually did it.

But as the adrenaline fades, I realize our job is far from over. Paul's plan is still in motion, and we're the only ones who can stop it.

"Alright," I say, straightening up and surveying the vault. "We've bought ourselves some time, but we're not out of the woods yet. Paul's plan is still unfolding, and we need to shut it down for good."

Gary nods, his nozzle set in a determined line. "So what's the play, boss? How do we undo whatever that twisted paperclip has set in motion?"

I turn to the rows of filing cabinets lining the vault walls. Each one is filled with enough secrets to topple governments or rewrite history. It's a sobering reminder of the life I left behind.

"We need to find Paul's master plan," I explain, already moving towards the nearest cabinet. "He must have left some trace of his endgame here. Carl, can you use your navigation skills to help us narrow down the search?"

Carl's needle begins to glow softly as he concentrates. "I'm sensing a strong concentration of recent activity in the northwest corner. That might be our best bet."

We split up, rifling through files and documents with frantic energy. The clock is ticking, and every second brings Paul's plan closer to fruition.

"Hey, I think I found something!" Gary calls out after what feels like hours but is probably only minutes.

We crowd around him as he spreads out a series of documents on a nearby table. Schematics, code sequences, and what looks like a manifesto written in Paul's distinctive scrawl.

"'Project Rewrite,'" I read aloud, my eyes widening as I scan the contents. "Paul wasn't just after control of the stationery world. He's trying to rewrite reality itself."

Carl leans in, his needle twitching as he absorbs the information. "It appears he's created a network of information nodes across the globe. By manipulating the data at these key points, he can effectively change how people perceive and interact with the world."

"But how is that even possible?" Gary asks, his voice tinged with disbelief.

I shake my head, the full scope of Paul's plan becoming clear. "In today's world, information is everything. Control the flow of data, and you control reality. Paul's using my old intel as a foundation, but he's taken it to a whole new level."

We pore over the documents, piecing together the intricate web Paul has woven. It's brilliant, in a terrifying sort of way. Every major information hub, every key decision-maker – they're all unwitting pawns in his grand design.

"So how do we stop it?" Gary asks, voicing the question we're all thinking.

I straighten up, a plan starting to form in my mind. "We fight fire with fire. Paul's using information as a weapon? Well, so can we."

I move to an old computer terminal in the corner of the vault, blowing off a layer of dust as I boot it up. "This system isn't connected to any outside network. It's completely isolated, which means Paul couldn't have tampered with it."

My fingers fly over the keyboard as I access old protocols and security measures I'd hoped never to use again. "We're going to create a countermeasure. A virus, of sorts, that will seek out and neutralize Paul's information nodes."

Carl's needle spins excitedly. "A brilliant strategy, Pete. But how do we ensure it targets only Paul's network without causing collateral damage?"

I allow myself a grim smile. "That's where you come in, old friend. Your innate sense of direction, combined with the data we've uncovered here, should allow us to create a targeted strike."

For the next hour, we work feverishly to construct our digital weapon. Gary keeps watch, ready to alert us to any signs of Paul's minions discovering our survival. Carl interfaces directly with the computer, his unique abilities allowing us to fine-tune our virus to an unprecedented degree.

As for me, I draw on every ounce of my past experience, every dirty trick and backdoor I ever created. It's a part of myself I'd tried to leave behind, but now, it might be our only hope of saving the world.

Finally, with a series of complex keystrokes, our countermeasure is ready. I sit back, feeling a mixture of pride and trepidation.

"This is it," I say, my voice hoarse from hours of intense focus. "Once we activate this, there's no going back. It'll spread through Paul's network like wildfire, dismantling his control and exposing his plan to the world."

Gary places a supportive hand on my shoulder. "We trust you, Pete. If anyone can pull this off, it's you."

Carl nods in agreement, his needle pointing steadily at the activation key. "The path is clear. It's time to right the wrongs and set the world back on its proper course."

I take a deep breath, savoring this moment of calm before the storm. Then, with a decisive click, I launch our digital countermeasure.

For a moment, nothing seems to happen. The computer hums quietly, lines of code scrolling across the screen faster than the eye can follow. Then, slowly but surely, we start to see the effects.

Alerts begin popping up on nearby monitors, showing Paul's network nodes going dark one by one. It's working. Our virus is cutting through his defenses like a hot knife through butter.

"We did it," Gary breathes, his voice filled with awe. "We actually did it!"

But our celebration is short-lived. A sudden tremor shakes the room, dust raining down from the ceiling.

"What was that?" I ask, already dreading the answer.

Carl's needle spins wildly, trying to pinpoint the source of the disturbance. "It seems Paul had one last failsafe in place. The entire facility is destabilizing!"

Another tremor, stronger this time, nearly knocks us off our feet. The reality of our situation sinks in – we've won the digital battle, but we're about to lose the physical one.

"We need to get out of here, now!" I shout, already moving towards the vault door. "This whole place is going to come down around our ears!"

We race through the crumbling facility, dodging falling debris and sparking electronics. The path that seemed so clear on our way in is now a treacherous obstacle course.

"Almost there!" I call out as we near the hidden staircase. "Just a little further!"

But fate, it seems, has one last cruel twist in store for us. As we reach the base of the stairs, a massive support beam comes crashing down, blocking our escape route.

"No!" Gary cries out, frantically trying to shift the beam. "We're so close!"

I look around desperately, searching for another way out. But the walls are closing in, the floor beneath us groaning with the strain.

In that moment, I realize what needs to be done. It's not a decision I make lightly, but it's the only way to ensure that everything we've fought for wasn't in vain.

"Gary, Carl," I say, my voice calm despite the chaos around us. "I need you to listen carefully. There's a maintenance shaft behind that far wall. It's a tight squeeze, but it leads to the surface."

Gary's eyes widen as he realizes what I'm saying. "No. No way, Pete. We're not leaving you behind!"

I shake my head, a sad smile on my face. "Someone needs to stay and make sure the countermeasure completes its work. Besides, I built this place. If anyone has a chance of finding another way out, it's me."

Carl's needle droops, but he nods in understanding. "Your path is clear, old friend. We'll make sure your sacrifice isn't in vain."

Another violent tremor emphasizes the urgency of the situation. There's no time for long goodbyes or dramatic speeches.

"Go!" I shout, giving them a push towards the hidden shaft. "And whatever happens, don't look back!"

As Gary and Carl disappear into the narrow passage, I turn back to face my old hideout one last time. The place where Pencil Pete was born, and where he might very well meet his end.

But as the walls crumble around me and the floor begins to give way, I feel a strange sense of peace. We've stopped Paul's plan. We've saved the world. And in doing so, I've finally found a way to atone for my past.

The last thing I see before the darkness closes in is a bright flash of light. Whether it's the facility's final death throes or something more... well, I suppose that's a story for another day.

After all, every good tale needs a little mystery, doesn't it?

7 The Final Draft

43

The neon sign flickered weakly, casting an eerie glow over the rain-slicked streets. I adjusted my grip on the steering wheel, my eraser leaving smudges on the worn leather. The wipers squeaked a melancholy rhythm as I pulled up to the curb, killing the engine with a weary sigh.

My old hideout loomed before me, a derelict monument to a past I'd tried so hard to erase. But some things, it seemed, refused to be forgotten. I slipped out of the car, the cool night air carrying the scent of impending doom.

"You sure about this, Pete?" Glue Gun Gary's gruff voice crackled through my earpiece. "Smells like a trap to me."

I chuckled darkly. "When doesn't it, old friend? Keep your nozzle warm. I might need that sticky touch of yours before the night's through."

"Just don't do anything stupid," Compass Carl chimed in, his calm tone a stark contrast to the tension thrumming through my lead. "Remember, true north isn't always where you think it is."

"Save the fortune cookie wisdom for later, Carl," I muttered, approaching the building's entrance. "I've got a date with destiny, and she doesn't like to be kept waiting."

The door creaked open at my touch, years of neglect evident in its rusty protest. I slipped inside, my senses on high alert. The air was thick with dust and memories, each step stirring up ghosts I'd long since buried.

As I descended into the bowels of my former sanctuary, a familiar voice slithered through the darkness. "Welcome home, Graphite Gray. Or should I say... Pencil Pete?"

I froze, my lead running cold. There, amidst piles of scattered documents and artifacts from my checkered past, stood Paperclip Paul. His silver form gleamed menacingly in the dim light, a cruel smile etched across his face.

"Paul," I growled, my hand instinctively reaching for the concealed eraser at my hip. "I see you've made yourself comfortable. Didn't your mother teach you it's rude to go through other people's things?"

He laughed, a sound like nails on a chalkboard. "Oh, Pete. Always with the quips. But I'm afraid your wit won't save you this time. You see, I know everything now. Every dirty little secret, every life you've erased. And with this—" he held up my manuscript, waving it tauntingly, "—I'll control not just your future, but the entire stationery underworld."

I took a step forward, my voice low and dangerous. "Put it down, Paul. You have no idea what you're dealing with."

"Oh, but I do," he sneered. "I've spent years piecing together your past, unraveling the mystery of the infamous Graphite Gray. And now, I'm going to erase you from history. Poetic, isn't it? The great assassin, reduced to nothing more than a smudge on the page."

My mind raced, searching for a way out of this mess. Paul had me cornered, surrounded by the very secrets I'd fought so hard to keep buried. But as I stared into his smug face, something inside me snapped.

"You want to know the truth, Paul?" I snarled, my body coiling like a spring. "The truth is, you're nothing but a second-rate fastener with delusions of grandeur. And I'm about to show you why they called me the deadliest writing implement in the business."

With lightning speed, I whipped out my eraser, firing off a barrage of rubber shavings that sent Paul diving for cover. He may have known my past, but he'd forgotten one crucial detail: I was still the best damn pencil in the game.

The room erupted into chaos as Paul's minions swarmed from the shadows. Staplers clicked menacingly, their metal jaws snapping at my heels. I vaulted over a desk, my body moving with fluid grace honed by years of training and survival.

A hulking hole punch lumbered towards me, its massive fists promising a world of pain. I ducked under its wild swing, using its momentum to send it crashing into a filing cabinet. The sound of crunching metal filled the air as drawers burst open, spewing their contents across the floor.

"Gary!" I shouted into my earpiece, narrowly avoiding a spray of pushpins. "Could use some of that sticky situation management right about now!"

"On it, boss!" came the reply, followed by the distinctive sound of adhesive weaponry being prepped.

I grinned, despite the dire circumstances. It was time to even the odds.

With a thunderous crash, Glue Gun Gary burst through a boarded-up window, his nozzle blazing with molten fury. Globs of adhesive flew through the air, pinning unsuspecting foes to walls and floors alike.

"Thought you could use a hand, Pete," Gary quipped, his gruff exterior betraying a hint of excitement. "Or should I say, a stick?"

I groaned at the pun, but there was no denying the lift in my spirits. "Just like old times, eh Gary? Try not to enjoy this too much."

As we fought back-to-back, a calm voice cut through the din of battle. "Gentlemen, if I may suggest a more strategic approach?"

Compass Carl stepped into view, his polished brass form gleaming with quiet confidence. With a few deft movements, he began redirecting our efforts, his innate sense of direction proving invaluable in the chaotic melee.

"Pete, three o'clock!" Carl called out. I spun, my eraser finding its mark and rubbing out a sneaking paper clip before it could strike.

"Gary, cover that exit!" Another spray of glue sealed off a potential escape route for Paul's minions.

As the tide of battle turned in our favor, I caught sight of Paul making a break for it, my manuscript clutched in his grasp. With a burst of speed, I gave chase, vaulting over upended furniture and dodging the last desperate attacks of his dwindling forces.

"Oh no, you don't," I muttered, my focus narrowing to a laser point. This ends now.

I cornered Paul in what used to be my old study, the room where I'd penned countless tales of adventure and intrigue. How fitting that it should be the stage for this final confrontation.

"It's over, Paul," I said, my voice steady despite the adrenaline coursing through me. "Drop the manuscript and surrender."

He backed away, his bravado crumbling in the face of defeat. "You don't understand, Pete. I had to do it. They made me! There are forces at work here beyond your imagination!"

I raised an eyebrow, my eraser trained on his quivering form. "Save it for the recycling bin, Paul. Whatever game you're playing, it ends here."

With a desperate cry, Paul lunged at me, the manuscript raised like a shield. Time seemed to slow as I sidestepped his clumsy attack, my body moving with the precision of a well-oiled machine. In one fluid motion, I disarmed him, sending the precious document flying across the room.

Paul stumbled, off-balance and vulnerable. I seized the opportunity, delivering a swift series of strikes that left him crumpled on the floor, thoroughly defeated.

As the dust settled, Gary and Carl joined me, surveying the scene with a mix of relief and wariness.

"Nice work, Pete," Gary said, giving me a congratulatory pat on the back that nearly knocked me over. "Guess you haven't lost your touch after all."

I allowed myself a small smile, the weight of years lifting from my shoulders. "Couldn't have done it without you two. Now, let's secure that manuscript and get out of here. I've had enough trips down memory lane for one lifetime."

As I retrieved the battered document, a sense of closure washed over me. The secrets of my past were safe, and with them, the lives I'd worked so hard to protect.

But as we turned to leave, a chill ran down my spine. There, in the doorway, stood a figure shrouded in shadow. Before any of us could react, a voice like silk over steel cut through the air.

"Well done, Graphite Gray. But I'm afraid your little victory celebration is premature. The game, as they say, has only just begun."

The figure melted back into the darkness, leaving us with more questions than answers. I exchanged worried glances with Gary and Carl, the realization sinking in that our troubles were far from over.

"Well, boys," I said, trying to inject some levity into the suddenly tense atmosphere, "looks like the pen isn't just mightier than the sword—it's also better at tying up loose ends. And from the looks of it, we've got a whole spool to untangle."

As we made our way out of the building, the weight of the manuscript in my hand felt heavier than ever. Whatever challenges lay ahead, I knew one thing for certain: our story was far from over.

8 The Final Act

The rain had intensified, turning the city into a shimmering maze of neon reflections and deep shadows. I clutched the manuscript to my chest, my mind reeling from the mysterious figure's ominous words. Gary and Carl flanked me, their usual banter replaced by a tense silence.

"So, what's the play, Pete?" Gary finally asked as we reached the relative safety of my battered sedan. "We just gonna pretend that whole creepy shadow routine didn't happen?"

I sighed, running a hand over my worn surface. "Much as I'd like to, old friend, I've got a feeling ignoring this particular problem isn't an option."

Carl's calm voice cut through the patter of rain on metal. "Perhaps we should seek higher ground. Both literally and figuratively. A change in perspective often reveals hidden truths."

I nodded, an idea forming. "You're right, Carl. And I know just the place. Buckle up, boys. We're taking a little road trip."

The engine roared to life, and we peeled away from the curb, leaving the scene of our recent victory behind. As we navigated the rain-slicked streets, my mind wandered back to the mysterious figure and their cryptic warning.

"You really think Paul was just a pawn?" Gary mused, his reflection in the rearview mirror betraying a hint of concern. "I mean, the guy's always been a few paperclips short of a full box, but this seems a bit much, even for him."

I gripped the steering wheel tighter, my knuckles turning white. "I don't know, Gary. But whoever's pulling the strings, they've got resources we can't even imagine. We need to be ready for anything."

The city gave way to winding mountain roads, the lights of civilization fading behind us. After what felt like hours of hairpin turns and steep climbs, we finally reached our destination: a long-abandoned lookout point that had once served as my personal sanctuary.

As we stepped out of the car, the cool mountain air cleared my head. The view was breathtaking, the city spread out below us like a glittering carpet of light. But I hadn't come here for the scenery.

"Alright, Pete," Carl said, his usual serenity tinged with urgency. "We're here. Now what?"

I took a deep breath, steeling myself for what came next. "Now, we prepare. Whatever's coming, we face it together. But first, there's something you both need to know."

I opened the manuscript, flipping to a dog-eared page near the back. "This isn't just a novel. It's a code. Every seemingly innocent story, every character... they're all part of a larger puzzle. One that, if solved, could shake the very foundations of the stationery world."

Gary's eyes widened. "You mean..."

I nodded grimly. "That's right. This manuscript contains the locations of every hidden cache, every secret alliance, and every skeleton in the closet of the major players in our little underground. In the wrong hands, it could spark a war that would make our recent scuffle look like a schoolyard tussle."

Carl stroked his polished surface thoughtfully. "And I assume our shadowy friend is after this information?"

"That'd be my guess," I replied, closing the manuscript with a snap. "Which is why we need to—"

My words were cut short by the distinctive whine of an incoming projectile. Years of honed instincts took over as I shouted, "Down!"

We dove for cover just as a barrage of razor-sharp paper airplanes sliced through the air where we'd been standing. I rolled behind a boulder, my heart pounding in my chest.

"Looks like the welcoming committee found us!" Gary yelled, returning fire with globs of quick-drying adhesive.

I risked a peek around my cover, assessing the situation. A small army of origami ninjas was advancing on our position, their paper forms fluttering menacingly in the mountain breeze. Behind them, a familiar figure emerged from the shadows, her pristine white form gleaming in the moonlight.

"Whiteout Wendy," I growled, ducking back as a shuriken made of sharpened Post-it notes whistled past my head. "Should've known she'd be involved in this mess."

"Pete!" Carl called out, his usually calm demeanor replaced by urgent focus. "We're outnumbered and outgunned. We need a plan!"

I wracked my brain, searching for a solution. The manuscript weighed heavily in my pocket, a constant reminder of what was at stake. Then, like a bolt of lightning, inspiration struck.

"Gary!" I shouted over the din of battle. "Remember that trick we pulled in Buenos Aires? The one with the improvised flamethrower?"

A wicked grin spread across Gary's face. "Oh yeah, boss. I'm picking up what you're putting down."

I turned to Carl. "I need you to calculate the exact angle and force needed to hit Wendy's troops with maximum effect. Can you do that?"

Carl's eyes gleamed with determination. "Consider it done, my friend."

As Carl began his rapid-fire calculations, Gary and I set to work. Using spare parts from the car and Gary's seemingly endless supply of adhesive, we cobbled together a makeshift weapon that looked more like a child's science project than an instrument of destruction.

"You sure about this, Pete?" Gary asked as we put the finishing touches on our contraption. "One wrong move and we could end up as kindling ourselves."

I clapped him on the shoulder, a grim smile on my face. "When has that ever stopped us before? Besides, I've got a few tricks left up my sleeve. Or should I say, up my barrel?"

With a nod to Carl, we sprang into action. Gary manned our jury-rigged flamethrower, unleashing a torrent of burning adhesive that sent the origami forces scattering in panic. I used the chaos to make a break for Wendy, my body moving with a grace and power I thought I'd left behind years ago.

Wendy's eyes widened in surprise as I closed the distance between us. "You!" she snarled, her brush dripping with corrosive whiteout. "I should have known you'd be too stubborn to die!"

I dodged her first strike, feeling the burn of whiteout as it grazed my surface. "What can I say, Wendy? I've always been hard to erase."

We traded blows, our forms blurring with the speed and intensity of our combat. Wendy was good, I had to give her that. But she'd forgotten one crucial detail: I wasn't just fighting for myself anymore.

With a move that would have made my old sensei proud, I feinted left before dropping low, sweeping Wendy's legs out from under her. She hit the ground hard, her brush clattering away uselessly.

I stood over her, my eraser poised for the final strike. "It's over, Wendy. Tell me who you're working for, and maybe we can end this without any more bloodshed."

Wendy's laughter caught me off guard, a sound of genuine amusement rather than defeat. "Oh, Pencil Pete. You really don't get it, do you? This was never about you, or that manuscript, or even control of the underworld. We're all just pawns in a game so much bigger than you can imagine."

Before I could press her further, a blinding light engulfed us. The thrumming of helicopter blades filled the air as a spotlight pinned us in place. From the chopper's open door, a figure rappelled down, landing with catlike grace between Wendy and me.

My lead ran cold as I recognized the newcomer: Tape Tom, the most feared enforcer in the stationery world. His adhesive form glistened menacingly in the harsh light.

"Well, well, well," Tom drawled, his voice dripping with malice. "Isn't this a touching reunion? The prodigal pencil returns, thinking he can erase the past with a few clever moves and witty one-liners."

I'll continue the chapter from where we left off:

Tom's eyes glinted dangerously as he circled us, his adhesive form uncoiling with predatory grace. "You know, Pete, I've been waiting for this moment for a long time. The chance to finally bind you up and make sure you never escape your past again."

I tensed, my grip tightening on my trusty eraser. "Sorry to disappoint you, Tom, but I'm not the binding type. I prefer to keep my options... flexible."

With lightning speed, Tom lashed out, a strip of razor-sharp tape slicing through the air where my head had been a split second before. I ducked and rolled, feeling the rush of displaced air as his attack missed by mere millimeters.

"Gary! Carl! A little help here?" I called out, narrowly avoiding another of Tom's vicious swipes.

"Kind of busy at the moment, boss!" Gary's strained voice carried over the chaos. He and Carl were fending off a renewed assault from the origami forces, their makeshift flamethrower sputtering as it ran low on fuel.

I cursed under my breath, realizing I was on my own for this dance. Tom pressed his advantage, his relentless attacks forcing me on the defensive. Each movement was a calculated risk, a deadly game of cat and mouse played out on the edge of a cliff.

"You've lost your edge, Pete," Tom taunted, his adhesive limbs stretching and contorting in ways that defied physics. "All those years playing at being a writer have made you soft. It's time someone put you back in your place – stuck to the page where you belong!"

His words stung more than I cared to admit, striking at the heart of my deepest fears. Had I really lost my touch? Was I nothing more than a washed-up has-been, clinging to delusions of redemption?

But as Tom's tape wrapped around my arm, threatening to immobilize me, something snapped inside. A fire I thought long extinguished roared to life, fueled by determination and the realization of how far I'd come.

"You're right about one thing, Tom," I growled, my voice low and dangerous. "I'm not the same pencil I used to be. I'm better."

With a surge of strength, I twisted free of his grip, using the momentum to deliver a devastating counterstrike. My sharpened point found its mark, leaving a deep gouge in Tom's adhesive hide.

He howled in pain and rage, his cool demeanor cracking. "You'll pay for that, you graphite gnat!"

Our battle intensified, a blur of strikes, parries, and near-misses that pushed us both to our limits. I could feel my lead wearing thin, each exertion bringing me closer to the breaking point. But I refused to give in, drawing on reserves of strength I didn't know I possessed.

As we grappled at the edge of the cliff, the helicopter's spotlight casting harsh shadows across the battlefield, I caught a glimpse of something that changed everything. There, half-hidden in the shadows of the chopper's open door, was a figure I recognized all too well.

"No," I whispered, momentarily stunned by the revelation. "It can't be..."

Tom seized on my distraction, his adhesive form coiling around me like a python. "Game over, Pete," he sneered, tightening his grip. "Time to face the music."

But even as the air was squeezed from my lungs, my mind raced. The pieces of the puzzle were falling into place, revealing a picture far more complex and terrifying than I'd imagined.

With a herculean effort, I twisted in Tom's grasp, bringing my mouth close to his ear. "You want to know the truth, Tom? The real reason I left the game all those years ago?"

His grip loosened slightly, curiosity getting the better of him. "What are you babbling about?"

I smiled grimly, knowing I was about to change the rules of engagement forever. "It's all in the manuscript. Every dirty secret, every backroom deal, every skeleton in the closet of the stationery world's elite. Including the identity of the one pulling all the strings."

Tom's eyes widened, a flicker of fear crossing his face. "You're bluffing."

"Am I?" I countered, my voice steady despite the pressure on my chest. "Why don't you ask your boss up there in the chopper? I'm sure they'd be very interested to know that their most trusted enforcer is having doubts."

The seed of doubt I'd planted took root, and I felt Tom's grip slacken ever so slightly. It was all the opening I needed.

With a move that would have made my old sensei proud, I broke free of Tom's hold, using his own momentum to send him stumbling towards the cliff's edge. He teetered on the brink, arms windmilling as he fought for balance.

"Pete, don't—" he gasped, genuine fear replacing his earlier bravado.

For a moment, I was tempted to let him fall, to end this chapter of my life once and for all. But that wasn't who I was anymore. With a sigh, I reached out, grabbing Tom's adhesive arm and pulling him back from the precipice.

"Consider us even," I said, my voice tinged with exhaustion and a hint of grudging respect.

As Tom slumped to the ground, the sound of slow, mocking applause filled the air. The mysterious figure from the helicopter had finally decided to show themselves, rappelling down to join us on the clifftop.

"Bravo, Pencil Pete," a voice smooth as silk and sharp as a paper cut called out. "You always did have a flair for the dramatic. It's part of what made you such an effective... instrument... in our organization."

I turned slowly, steeling myself for the confrontation I'd been both dreading and anticipating for years. "Hello, Eraserhead," I said, facing the mastermind behind it all. "It's been a long time."

Eraserhead, the shadowy leader of the stationery underworld, stood before me in all his rubberized glory. His featureless face betrayed no emotion, but I could feel the weight of his gaze boring into me.

"Indeed it has, my old friend," Eraserhead replied, his tone maddeningly casual. "I must say, retirement seems to have suited you well. Your skills are as sharp as ever."

I clenched my fists, fighting to keep my composure. "Cut the small talk, Eraserhead. What's this all about? Why drag me back into a world I left behind?"

He chuckled, the sound sending chills down my spine. "Oh, Pete. You never truly left. You've been playing your part all along, whether you realized it or not. The manuscript, the friends you've made, even your little adventures in the world of literature – it's all been part of a grand design."

My mind reeled, struggling to process the implications of his words. "What are you saying?"

Eraserhead spread his arms wide, encompassing the chaos of the battlefield around us. "I'm saying, my dear Pencil Pete, that it's time for the final act. The stationery world is on the brink of a revolution, and you're going to help us usher in a new era – whether you like it or not."

As the weight of his words sank in, I realized that my greatest challenge was yet to come. The battle for my soul – and the fate of the entire stationery world – was only just beginning.

Certainly. I'll continue the story, working towards a resolution that aligns with the original outline:

The weight of Eraserhead's words hung in the air, heavy as lead. I stood my ground, mind racing to process this earth-shattering revelation. Gary and Carl, having finally subdued the last of the origami forces, joined me, their faces etched with concern and confusion.

"You've got it all wrong, Eraserhead," I said, my voice steadier than I felt. "I'm not playing any part in your grand design. Not anymore."

Eraserhead's featureless face somehow managed to convey amusement. "Oh, but you are, Pete. You always have been. Every word you've written, every life you've touched – it's all been leading to this moment."

I felt a hand on my shoulder and turned to see Carl, his compass face set with determination. "Whatever game you're playing," he said to Eraserhead, "Pete's not alone in this. We stand together."

"Yeah," Gary chimed in, his nozzle still smoking from the recent battle. "So why don't you take your cryptic nonsense and stick it where the sun don't shine?"

Eraserhead's chuckle sent chills down my spine. "Ah, the power of friendship. How quaint. But I'm afraid you're all out of your depth here. The manuscript, Pete. Hand it over, and perhaps we can discuss your role in the new world order I'm about to unleash."

My hand instinctively went to my pocket, feeling the weight of the document that had caused so much chaos. "And if I refuse?"

"Then I'm afraid things will get rather... messy," Eraserhead replied, his tone sickeningly sweet. With a snap of his fingers, a dozen more helicopters appeared on the horizon, their spotlights painting the cliffside in harsh white light.

I exchanged glances with Gary and Carl, seeing my own mix of fear and resolve mirrored in their eyes. We were outnumbered, outgunned, and running out of options. But I'd be damned if I was going to let Eraserhead win without a fight.

"You want the manuscript so badly?" I called out, pulling the document from my pocket. "Come and get it!"

With all my strength, I hurled the manuscript over the cliff's edge. Time seemed to slow as the pages fluttered in the wind, carrying with them the secrets of an entire underworld.

Eraserhead's cool demeanor finally cracked. "No!" he roared, lunging forward. But it was too late. The manuscript disappeared into the darkness below, lost to the night.

In the moment of stunned silence that followed, I made my move. With a nod to Gary and Carl, we sprang into action. Gary unleashed a torrent of adhesive, gumming up the rotors of the nearest helicopter. Carl, using his unerring sense of direction, guided us through the chaos towards our escape route.

As alarms blared and confusion reigned, we fought our way through Eraserhead's minions. It was a blur of motion – erasing here, sticking there, always moving forward. Despite the odds, we were making progress.

Just as we reached the edge of the fray, a familiar voice called out. "Pete! Catch!"

I turned to see Whiteout Wendy, of all people, tossing something in my direction. On instinct, I snatched it out of the air – a small, innocuous-looking USB drive.

"Insurance policy," she yelled over the din. "In case things went south. Now go!"

I hesitated for a split second, but the look in Wendy's eyes told me all I needed to know. With a nod of thanks, I pocketed the drive and rejoined Gary and Carl in our mad dash for freedom.

We reached my battered sedan just as Eraserhead's forces regrouped. Tires squealing, we peeled away from the scene, the sounds of pursuit fading into the distance as we navigated the treacherous mountain roads.

As the adrenaline began to wear off, the reality of what had just transpired started to sink in. "So," Gary said, breaking the tense silence, "anyone want to explain what the hell just happened back there?"

I sighed, my grip on the steering wheel loosening slightly. "I wish I knew, Gary. But something tells me we've just scratched the surface of a conspiracy bigger than anything we could have imagined."

Carl's calm voice cut through the tension. "Perhaps the answers lie in that drive Wendy gave you, Pete. It seems we have an unexpected ally in this fight."

I nodded, my mind already racing with possibilities. "You're right, Carl. But whatever's on this drive, I have a feeling it's going to change everything."

As we wound our way down the mountain, the first rays of dawn began to peek over the horizon. The new day brought with it a mix of uncertainty and hope – and the knowledge that our adventure was far from over.

"Well, boys," I said, a wry smile tugging at the corner of my mouth, "looks like the pen isn't just mightier than the sword – it's also better at tying up loose ends. And from the looks of it, we've got a whole spool to untangle."

Gary groaned at the pun, but I could see the glimmer of excitement in his eyes. "So what's the plan, boss? We going to take on the entire stationery underworld with just the three of us?"

I chuckled, feeling a familiar thrill coursing through my lead. "Why not? We've got brains, brawn, and an unerring moral compass. What more could we need?"

As we drove off into the sunrise, I couldn't help but feel that this was just the beginning of a much larger story. Whatever challenges lay ahead, whatever secrets that USB drive held, I knew one thing for certain: with friends like these by my side, we stood a fighting chance.

The road stretched out before us, full of promise and peril. And I, Pencil Pete, ex-assassin turned novelist turned reluctant hero, was ready to write the next chapter – not just in my books, but in the very fabric of the stationery world itself.

THE END... FOR NOW

ABOUT THE AUTHOR

An explorer of stories and a lover of adventure, Amy creates tales that blend action, humor, and heart. She believes in the power of fiction to inspire and entertain. Lead and Let Die is the latest creation, offering readers a thrilling escape into a world of imagination. With a background that includes various creative pursuits,she brings a fresh perspective to the world of young adult fiction. Amy invites readers to dive into the adventures of Lead and Let Die and explore the limitless possibilities of imagination. She lives in India and continues to craft new stories.